MATTHEW'S GOALS

This edition published 2010
First published 1997 by
A & C Black Publishers Ltd
36 Soho Square, London, W1D 3QY

www.acblack.com

Text copyright © 1997 Michael Hardcastle
Illustrations copyright © 1997 Bob Moulder
Cover illustration copyright © 2010 Maya Gavin

The rights of Michael Hardcastle and Bob Moulder to be
identified as author and illustrator of this work respectively
have been asserted by them in accordance with the
Copyrights, Designs and Patents Act 1988.

ISBN 978-1-4081-2233-4

A CIP catalogue for this book is available
from the British Library.

This book is produced using paper that is made from wood
grown in managed, sustainable forests. It is natural, renewable and
recyclable. The logging and manufacturing processes conform to the
environmental regulations of the country of origin.

Printed and bound in China by C&C Offset Printing.

MATTHEW'S GOALS

Michael Hardcastle

Illustrated by Bob Moulder

A & C Black • London

CHAPTER ONE

Milan come again with Baresi...

MATTHEW!

His mother's voice powered through the doorway and swamped the sounds of the football match on the DVD. 'Down here – now!'

Matthew hesitated. There was a good goal coming up.

...to Albertini...

Just coming.

MATTHEW! Come down here immediately – or there'll be trouble!

Matthew bolted down the stairs, two at a time.

He couldn't imagine what was wrong, but he knew that tone of voice and it always meant trouble. Mum was waiting by the kitchen door, eyes blazing. It had to be a hanging offence.

Suddenly, he knew what the trouble was.

You've done it again. AGAIN! After all your promises. It'll cost us a fortune!

Oh no ... not the freezer!

Oh *yes*. I can't believe it! You've left the door open again. How could you? I've just spent hundreds of pounds re-stocking it. Now everything's ruined.

Matthew was speechless. How on earth was he going to get out of this? Whatever he said, he knew it would not calm his mother. How could he have been so forgetful?

9

CHAPTER TWO

Matthew sat on the end of his bed, gazing unseeingly out of the window. He still couldn't believe it – this was the second time he'd left the freezer door open in three months. It had been bad enough last time, he'd had his pocket money stopped for six weeks, but now it had cost him a vital football match.

His brother, Eddie, hovered in the doorway.

It's just the end of the world, isn't it?

13

Mum, however, was on the phone in her bedroom and at that moment she wasn't the slightest bit interested in what her sons were doing. All the same, the boys crept out of the house like thieves and headed down the garden path which was strewn with damp leaves after recent gales and floods. They climbed over the fence into the muddy lane, and followed its twists and turns until they reached a wide, flat patch of ground surrounded by ancient trees.

It was a brilliant place for practising.

The two boys rained shots at the trees for as long as they had energy. The ball bounced back at angles for them to trap or volley against another target.

Rashwood aren't going to win without your goals. Can't you ask Tiger Johnson to help?

16

CHAPTER THREE

With four days to go before the Cup tie, and still no sign of Mum changing her mind, Eddie decided to tackle Tiger Johnson. Luckily, he had P.E. with Tiger that morning, and he waited patiently for his chance. He had been on the trampoline for what seemed ages before Mr Johnson came over to pass some comments on his style and the height he'd achieved.

Sir, you've got to listen. You're our only hope. Matthew's going out of his mind with worry. And Rashwood desperately need his goals, don't they?

The P.E. teacher sighed.

Eddie, you've got to stop this.
Your mother's decision is the only one
that matters. Tackle her, not me. Now...

Eddie had tried his best; now
he had to try something else.

Well, if Matthew can't play, can
I play in his place? I mean,
I score goals too. Good ones.

Mr Johnson shook his head in disbelief.

Good of you
to offer, Eddie,
but no chance.
You're, er, not
tall enough.

I'll grow.

Mr Johnson tried not to smile.

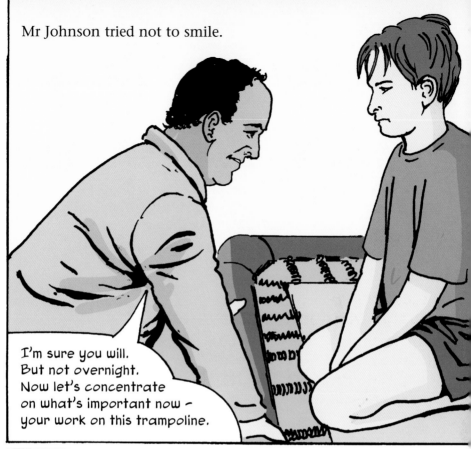

I'm sure you will.
But not overnight.
Now let's concentrate
on what's important now –
your work on this trampoline.

At morning break, Eddie caught up with Matthew.

I tried to talk to Tiger, but he
won't listen to me. You've got
to speak to him, Matthew.

OK, I'll give it a go, but
I bet it won't do any good.

It was lunchtime before Matthew caught up with Tiger Johnson. He was jogging onto the pitch to take charge of a football match.

Mr Johnson, please, you've got to help me. You've...

No chance, Matthew. I've already told your brother that your mother deserves my support, and I've given her my word.

Matthew walked away in despair. He was convinced he'd never score another goal in his life.

Suddenly, the ball flew towards him from a miskick on the pitch. Without thinking, he swung his leg to send it back, and missed the ball completely –

The laughter which followed him as he walked away was so embarrassing he made no effort to retrieve the ball. His nightmare was getting worse by the minute.

CHAPTER FOUR

Matthew worked hard all weekend to try to please his mother. On Sunday morning, when he should have been playing for his league side in an away fixture, he was busy painting the fence at the rear of the garden. His mother had pointed out that it needed to be done and Matthew reacted with speed. He was prepared to do almost any chore to win his mother over. Although his brain told him she wouldn't lift the ban, his heart persuaded him there must be a chance if he kept doing helpful things.

The sudden appearance of three of his classmates, Oliver, Rebecca and Karl, took him completely by surprise.

Hey, what are you doing here?

He hoped his embarrassment wasn't too obvious – surely his friends wouldn't tell everyone that Matthew Leaman spent Sunday morning painting a fence?

We've come to see your mother.

His friends didn't allow their faces to crack into a grin,
let alone a smile.

Oliver announced:

Matthew swung round. His mum had arrived and was leaning forward on a spade she'd been using in the front garden. He recognised the determination behind the pose.

If you've come to try and spirit Matthew away to a football match, forget it. His playing days are staying in the deep freeze where our food supplies should be.

Matthew surprised himself by what he did next.

I've had enough of this. Let's get out of here. Let's have some fun.

His mother fired a parting shot as they all headed for the gate.

Just remember the ban, Matthew. And make sure you're back by two o'clock – we've got some shopping to do.

29

After checking they had enough money, they caught a bus into town and made their way to Top Strike Bowling.

Matthew was just putting on his bowling shoes when he heard a voice behind him.

I see you're taking up a new game, Leaman. Very wise of you – by the time your football ban is over, I'll have taken your place in the school team, and you'll never get it back!

Matthew recognised the voice immediately – Ashley Kennard, a spiky-haired player who always had a high opinion of himself as a footballer. In fact, his skills were limited but he always blamed his poor progress on his frequent injuries.

Grow up, Ashes. You'll never be big enough to take my place in anything. Anyway, I thought you'd damaged your ankle.

It's getting better by the minute. You can't say the same about your chances of playing again though, can you? They seem to be getting worse by the minute.

Matthew watched him walk away. Then, gritting his teeth, he picked up his bowl, stepped forward, swung his arm and hurled the bowl down the gleaming lane. Seven pins went down.

He felt a bit better – but not as good as he'd feel if he could only get back on to a soccer pitch and score a goal.

CHAPTER FIVE

As they came out of the supermarket, Matthew made another attempt to please his mum.

Whilst his mother sat behind the wheel of the car, Matthew unloaded the supermarket trolley.

Matthew piled all the bags into the boot and returned the trolley to its parking space.

CHAPTER SIX

It was raining again two days before the Cup tie was due to take place, but no one was complaining as the practice match entered its final ten minutes. Matthew paced up and down the touchline, full of nerves.

He didn't know what he wanted to happen: the school team to perform brilliantly without him, or his replacement, Tony, to miss a hatful of chances. Tony had already scorned two openings Matthew wouldn't have wasted with his eyes closed. Or so Matthew believed.

It hadn't occurred to him that an injury might suit him best – even in his most resentful moments he didn't want a team-mate to be hurt. But as soon as Tony fell, and fell awkwardly on his left arm, Matthew sensed that the injury was a bad one.

Tony had been running in to meet a cross, to aim a header just inside the near post. But he couldn't keep his footing on the greasy surface, and as he took off, his foot shot out from under him. Tony flung out an arm to save himself, but when he crashed down the pain was so dreadful he almost fainted.

Mr Johnson stopped the game immediately.

Another teacher who was watching came over.

I think he needs hospital treatment. Do you mind taking him?

No problem.

The other teacher gave Tony a quick examination.

It may not be as bad as you think. Some of these kids have amazing powers of recovery, you know.

I'll keep my fingers crossed.

Matthew didn't know what to say or think. But he had enough family loyalty to call out loudly:

He was aware that Eddie had been pestering Tiger for days on end to give him a chance in the team. Matthew supposed Tiger only put him on the bench to shut him up.

That first touch encouraged him, and a minute later he went off on a mazy dribble.

The clinging mud didn't seem to slow him down at all; he almost seemed to skip over it. The opposition were not expecting a one-man attack from a substitute, and backed off.

Even when Eddie surged into the penalty area, the goalie remained rooted to the spot.

Too late, he realised what Eddie intended – he moved out a couple of steps and was left helpless as Eddie fired the ball past him and into the net by the far post.

Well done, Eddie, well done!

At least Eddie was keeping up the family scoring record. But then a thought struck Matthew – how would he feel if Eddie were to keep him out of the Rashwood team when his playing ban was lifted?

A voice suddenly broke in on his thoughts.

Hey, Matt, I see your kid brother's playing now. But that goal was a fluke. I'll soon have his place when I'm fit to play again.

Matthew turned to see Ashley, his right arm in a sling following a fall from his bike.

Don't call me that! I'm not a mat that people wipe their feet on. It's Matthew, OK?

Well, OK, Matthew.

See you around, Matthew...

...amongst the spectators at the Cup tie.

Matthew watched him go, wishing he didn't feel in such a bad mood so much of the time.

At the end of school the following day, Matthew was talking about homework with Oliver and Becky when Eddie dashed up to them.

Have you heard the *good* news?

What news?

The Cup tie with Himbleton is *off* – postponed. Their pitch is waterlogged.

Nothing to do with me, Matthew felt like saying. But that wasn't true. He didn't know what to think.

How did you find out?

I met Tiger coming out of the secretary's office. He'd just had the phone call.

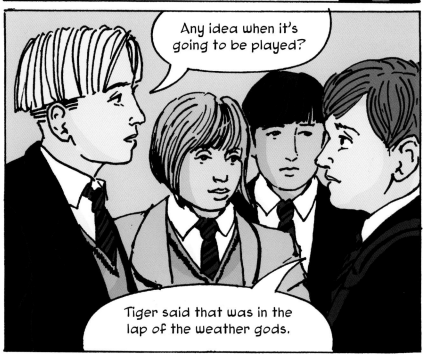

Any idea when it's going to be played?

Tiger said that was in the lap of the weather gods.

CHAPTER SEVEN

At six o'clock the following morning, Matthew was wide awake. The Himbleton match had been re-scheduled for the following week, so he still wouldn't be able to play.

He picked up a ball and let himself out of the silent house. It was a huge relief to get outside after lying awake for so long worrying about the match. It wasn't too cold, but there was dampness in the air and no sign of any stars.

He decided to stay in the garden, and began dribbling the ball around bushes and other obstacles.

He still needed to practise even if he wasn't playing in the Cup tie. Soon his enthusiasm got the better of him and he couldn't resist hitting a fierce shot against the garage door.

CLANG

YES!

The thump of the ball against the metal woke his father, who forced himself to get up and investigate.

What do you think you're doing? D'you know what time it is?

21 ... 22 ... 23 ... Er, about six?

Minutes later, Jeff Leaman slid back into bed beside his wife and told her what had happened.

We've got to give him a break. He's really suffering – mentally more than anything.

I think he's served his punishment now. And you said he's been helpful around the house.

True, but he hasn't missed a school match yet, has he, because of the postponement? So we've still got to think about that, Jeff. That's when it'll really hit him.

I'll think about it, but I'm not making any promises.

CHAPTER EIGHT

Himbleton's big central defender nodded the ball down as the cross came in, and his nearest team-mate hoofed the ball upfield.

Yet another Rashwood attack had failed and the home side remained in command with their 1-0 lead.

Matthew grabbed Tiger's arm.

How much longer,
Mr Johnson?

The coach glanced at his watch.

Matthew, it's only a couple of minutes since I
last told you; there's at least 25 minutes to go.
So, even if I wanted to, I can't put you on for
at least another five minutes. Just keep calm.

That was impossible. Now that he knew he was going to play again, he couldn't wait to get on the pitch. His parents had finally agreed that his ban should end; but that he could only play in the last quarter of the Himbleton Cup tie. He would be allowed on as a sub if the team needed him. So, for the first three-quarters of the game, Matthew had had to sit and suffer, watching his younger brother do his best to get a goal for Rashwood.

Himbleton kept up their attack and, suddenly, one of their strikers ran clear of the defence as the ball came to him.

Look out!
He's through.

Rashwood's goalie advanced and then, as he faced the attacker on the edge of the box, threw up his hand to keep the low sun out of his eyes.

That hesitation was fatal.

The Himbleton striker cracked the ball past the dazzled goalie into the net to double their lead.

Originally, it had been the rain that was Rashwood's enemy; now the sun seemed to have taken its place.

Oh no.

Matthew sensed that his chance of a Cup medal had disappeared. Tiger glanced at his watch.

Get ready, Matthew.

Tiger Johnson got to his feet, and signalled to the referee that he wanted to make a change.

On you go, Matthew. What's an extra minute!

He pushed Matthew onto the pitch.

Good luck.

The moment he got the ball, Matthew knew he had to show Himbleton what he could do; he had to terrify them, make them believe he could practically beat them on his own, cause panic in their defence. And it worked. Picking up a pass from Clive, he began a mazy run, turning this way then that, dragging his marker almost in a complete circle.

Eddie was calling for the ball, fearing that his brother hadn't even noticed where he was on the pitch.

But Matthew kept possession.

Then, without warning, he swerved again and headed straight for goal.

In despair, a full-back went for a tackle from behind.

Matthew stumbled and fell and the ball ran out of play. It should have been a foul, but instead the ref signalled a corner.

The kick was taken quickly, and when the ball reached him Matthew instinctively back-heeled it. Eddie, who was poaching by the far post, turned it into the net. It was the sort of trick they'd perfected during hours of training together.

Oh, great thinking, Matthew – that really fooled them!

It didn't arrive for twelve minutes. By this time, Matthew had two markers on him, so rather than go for glory himself, he decided to set up chances for the others. Eddie, who'd been tiring before scoring the first goal, seemed to have tapped new sources of energy. He ran at the Himbleton defence until, once again, a player fouled him on the edge of the box.

Matthew signalled to Clive, who then drifted away from the defensive wall. Deliberately, Matthew appeared to be aiming the free kick towards the opposite side of the box.

As the whistle sounded, he chipped it over to the left.

And Clive, darting in, headed the ball high into the net past the stranded goalkeeper.

What a goal!

Himbleton 2: Rashwood 2

Two minutes of the match remained. Tiger Johnson was dancing up and down with joy as well as worry.

Don't throw it away, boys!

In fact, neither side created a scoring chance, or conceded one, before the final whistle.

Well played, mate.

Thanks. See you at the replay I suppose.

But the ref explained that under the new rules, the teams would play extra time until a goal was scored – and that would be the end of the match.

Clive was still buzzing from his equalising goal as he took on the shaken Himbleton defence...

...but his cross was too high for Eddie, while Matthew, still marked by two opponents, couldn't get near it.

Eddie was the next to get in a shot after a neat flick-on from James, an adventurous midfielder.

Rashwood's band of supporters cheered loudly but still the goals wouldn't come. Time was running out – if the scores were still level after extra time, there'd be a penalty shoot-out. Whose nerves would cope with that?

Come on, Rashwood.

Suddenly, Eddie emerged from a scramble in midfield with the ball at his feet. He looked up, searching for Matthew. But Matthew, on the left, yelled:

As Eddie raced ahead, one of Matthew's markers peeled away to help deal with Eddie.

Eddie reached the edge of the box and whipped the ball across to the left.
It was just what Matthew had been hoping for as he accelerated like a sprinter.

His pace took him clear of everyone...

...except the goalkeeper.

Even before Matthew could try to take the ball round him,
the goalie flung himself headlong at the Rashwood attacker.
As Matthew went down under the assault, the shriek of the
ref's whistle told everyone what must happen next – a penalty!

77

Matthew took his time.

He could see how nervous the Himbleton goalkeeper was...

...and he had practised this shot hundreds of times. He took a short run towards the ball, swerved and...

Eddie was the first to embrace Matthew.